Silence In The Haze

Ovsanna Sinanyan

Dedication

I dedicate this book to all the young girls out there who are suffering from love. To those who have lost themselves in a relationship, I implore you: love yourself first and know your worth. Stop keeping everything to yourself, and prioritize your mental health by being more open and seeking help when needed.

Acknowledgment

It is with a sense of profound gratitude that I pen this acknowledgement. The creation of this novel was a journey of self-discovery and emotional exploration, one that would not have been possible without the unwavering support of those around me.

To my family, who provided a constant source of comfort and encouragement during the many long nights spent crafting this work, I offer my deepest thanks. Your love and understanding sustained me through the challenging moments and fueled my passion for storytelling.

To my friends, who offered their time and perspectives as I shared my ideas and sought guidance, I express my appreciation. Your insightful contributions and unwavering belief in my abilities inspired me to persevere and realize this vision.

To the men who created the stories that inspired this novel, I want to say a big thank you. I am grateful for this tragedy that fueled my memories and my past. Your actions may have caused me pain, but they have also given me the material to create something powerful and meaningful.

I also want to extend my gratitude to my therapist, Zara, and my project manager, who made it possible for me to share this work with the world. Your support and guidance have been instrumental in bringing this novel to life.

And finally, to the reader, I offer my sincerest appreciation. It is with humbled anticipation that I share this work with you, and I hope that it provides a source of inspiration, comfort, or even catharsis as you navigate your own journey.

Thank you, one and all, for playing a crucial role in the realization of this novel.

Contents

Dedication   iv

Acknowledgment   v

About the Author   viii

Preface   ix

Chapter 1: Meeting John   1

Chapter 2: First Times   10

Chapter 3: Here and There   20

Chapter 4: Secret Tales of a Drunk   27

Chapter 5: Forgive and Forget   37

Chapter 6: Is this Love?   46

Chapter 7: Therapy   57

Chapter 8: Finding Love   65

Chapter 9: Breaking the Rose-Colored Glasses   70

Chapter 10: No More   77

Chapter 11: On Fire   82

Chapter 12: The End   91

About the Author

Born on April 4, 2000, in the picturesque city of Sliven, Bulgaria, Ovsanna Sinanyan has lived a life of both cultural richness and personal resilience. The daughter of Armenian parents, she was raised in the rich cultural tapestry of Armenia and graduated from the esteemed Number 64 school in 2015. With a deep passion for the arts, she emigrated to the United States in pursuit of greater opportunities, eventually making her home in the vibrant city of Los Angeles. She graduated from Glendale high school in 2018. Ovsanna's talents extend beyond the canvas, as she holds a degree in Studio Art from Pasadena City College and is currently pursuing a bachelor's degree in Art Education from California State University, Northridge. She is a talented painter, driven by her own life experiences, and now, with the publication of her debut novel, she adds "author" to her impressive list of accomplishments. With her unique voice, Ovsanna has created a work that is both personal and universal, speaking to the complexities of the human experience and the resilience of the human spirit.

Preface

Allow me to paint a picture of a journey like no other.

This is the story of Anna, a woman who braves the tumultuous waters of heartbreak and rises like the phoenix from its ashes, emerging stronger and more radiant than ever before. As she transcends the boundaries of darkness and light, she embarks on a journey that symbolizes the passing of time - from Sunset to Sunrise.

With each step, she sheds her past like a cocoon and blossoms into a being of pure enlightenment. This is not merely a tale of survival, but a hymn to the human spirit and its unbreakable resolve. Through the pages of this hauntingly beautiful novel, we are privileged to bear witness to the metamorphosis of Anna, and to bask in the radiance of her newfound light.

Chapter 1: Meeting John

The smell of fresh brewing coffee invaded Anna's senses. It was like a warm hug on a cold winter morning. It brought an unconscious smile to her face as she nursed the warm mug in her freezing hands. She and her friends had been sitting in the coffee shop for a while now, but Anna's hands reused to warm up. she didn't mind, though. The porcelain mug with steaming light brown liquid was keeping her warm. She took another big whiff of her coffee before she tuned back into the conversation her friends had been indulging in for quite some time.

She focused her gaze on the group that surrounded her, and she felt another smile creep up her cheeks. Today was a good day. It was her high school graduation. Four years of blood, sweat, and tears had finally come to fruition. She was done with high school, and her friend shared her sentiments by shouting,

"WE'RE FINALLY FREE!"

Everyone joined in to cheer, and Anna raised her mug and laughed. She had a lot to be happy about. She was surrounded by the people she loved, her companions for the last four years, gathered around her like a warm fleece sweater protecting her from the harsh winter breeze. Their graduation had been nothing short of a fantasy, but it was over now, and things were beginning to get real. They had to think about what to do with their lives. The sudden realization dawned on Anna, and the smile that adorned her face fell into a slight frown.

"What are you guys thinking about doing now?" Anna asked her friends while fiddling with her coffee mug.

"I don't know. I was thinking that we could go for some dinner," one of them replied nonchalantly.

"No. I mean like a job. High school is over now. We probably need to get serious," Anna muttered.

A strange silence befell the group. The earlier chatter and laughter came to a sudden halt. Anna thought she had ruined everyone's mood, but one of her friends chirped up,

"Well, I was thinking of waitressing. It's easy, and it doesn't require a lot of skill. I could even work here," she pointed out, gesturing at the café around them.

"Waitressing? Hmm…I thought you wanted to study accounting?" Anna asked.

"Well, yes, but I'm gonna work for a year and save up some money for college. Plus, I really like this place. It's pretty and quiet," she replied.

Anna thought over her words. It seemed like a smart idea. Anna didn't have to worry about things like college because she wasn't planning on going. She had her art. Her lifeline. Anna had already devoted years of her life to perfecting her skill and her art. She wanted to take this free time to work on her exhibition. It was a far-fetched dream, but Anna knew that she could achieve it. She had the talent for it.

Anna's thoughts were disrupted by another one of her friends saying,

"If you want to work here, shouldn't you at least check if they're hiring waitresses?"

"Um…who do I ask? Her friend replied.

"We could see if the manager is here. I don't know who it is, but we can ask?" Anna replied.

Anna looked around, and her eyes fell on the cashier's counter, where they placed their order. For some reason, she was captured by the man leaning behind the counter fiddling with his phone. The first thing Anna noticed was that he was very handsome. He was a short man with a muscular build.

His hair was peculiar. It was black with heavy streaks of white and grey, reminding Anna of salt and pepper. His long beard framed his face well, and Anna recognized his designer clothes from her seat. The man had good style, and judging from his shiny shoes, he was well aware of the latest fashion trends.

It seemed Anna wasn't the only one who was intrigued by him because she heard her friends hoot and whistle quietly,

"Wow. Who is that hottie?" One of them giggled.

"How did we not notice him before," another one quipped.

Anna just smiled and kept her thoughts to herself. Instead, she said,

"We could ask him if they're hiring waitresses."

"Oh my god! Yes. I just need an excuse to get closer to him," the girl added.

Anna was already getting up from her seat and walking towards the counter with her friend behind her. The man noticed her coming, and it seemed that he was as intrigued by Anna as she was by him because he couldn't take his eyes off her.

"Hey, are you guys hiring?" Anna asked in a sweet voice with a flirty smile.

The man smiled back and spoke,

"Why? Do you want to work here?"

His voice was deep and sultry. Anna could tell he was older than her.

"No, but my friend was thinking about it," Anna said, pointing back to her group of friends who was star-struck by the man.

"Well, you can come back tomorrow for an interview, and then we'll see," he said, looking at Anna's friend, who almost fainted.

"Are you the manager?" Anna asked, eyebrows furrowed.

"Yeah, my name's John. Nice to meet you…?" he drifted off as if asking Anna for her name.

"Anna," she added with a smile, "Nice to meet you, John."

"It seemed like you girls were celebrating something." John continued the conversation.

"Yeah, we graduated high school today," Anna mentioned.

"Wow. I can't even remember my graduation. It was so long ago," John joked.

"Oh, yeah? How long?" Anna asked, intrigued.

"Well, I'm thirty-two, so you can do the math," he added.

"Wow, so you're like fourteen years older than me," Anna giggled. She knew he was older, but she didn't expect him to be that old. His looks deceived his age.

John only laughed and diverted the conversating back to my friend,

"Well, I'll see you tomorrow for the interview."

Anna's friend could only nod, and they rushed back to their table. Anna gave John one last look, and he had his eyes fixed on her too. Little did she know, this wasn't the last time she would see him.

A few months had passed since Anna's graduation. Time was flying by, and her paintings were coming along beautifully. Anna was really happy with her progress, and every time she finished a painting, she made a post on Instagram and shared it with her followers. She had made a public art account that she occasionally used for her personal pictures too, and her followers were growing day by day. Every time she shared her work, she gained new followers, and it made her feel so accomplished. With all of her artwork piling up, Anna didn't have the time to meet her friends, so she never got to know what happened with her friend's interview.

Speaking of interviews, Anna had completely forgotten about the attractive manager at the café. That was until that one fateful night when Anna's phone dinged with a new notification.

_John1990 wants to send you a message

Anna curiously peeked at her screen. She had been engrossed in another painting of hers, but the name made her reach out and unlock her phone. She had heard this name before, but she couldn't put her finger on it. she reluctantly clicked on the notification and saw the DM from this mysterious John,

"This is a masterpiece! You're incredibly talented, Anna."

That was strange. Her followers barely addressed her by name. she was a little creeped out, so she replied to the message,

"Do I know you?"

She received an instant reply,

"You don't remember me? That's strange. I couldn't forget you."

Anna's brows furrowed as she raked her brain for an answer. She knew this guy, but from where? Turned out that she didn't need to wonder for long because she received another message,

"It's John. From the café. Do you remember me?"

A light bulb went off in Anna's head, and it finally clicked. that's why his name sounded so familiar. She smiled sheepishly as she replied,

"Oh, you tracked me down? A little creepy, no?"

"No. No. Don't get me wrong. I came across your post, and I was instantly mesmerized. I couldn't take my eyes off it. When I saw your pictures on the account, I realized it was you. Crazy coincidence, right?"

Anna stared at John's text for a good minute. She didn't know why, but his compliments about her work made her heart flutter. She had gotten compliments from people before, but John's seemed so sincere. She started typing again,

"Thank you, John. It really means a lot. My art is everything to me, and I'm glad you liked it." Anna skipped out the part about her heart fluttering.

"You're not giving yourself enough credit! The way the colors blended together as one on the canvas. I felt like I could trace every brushstroke. I was lost in your art, Anna," John replied.

Anna felt blood rush to her cheeks. She had never heard anyone talk like this about her art. It was such a warm and wonderful feeling. He seemed like he had been observing her work for a while, and Anna couldn't help but be flattered.

"That's the sweetest thing anyone has ever said to me. I don't know what to say," she replied honestly, her heart rate increasing with every breath.

"Why don't we talk more about it over coffee? You seemed like you really enjoyed it at the café. You could stop by again," he suggested smoothly.

Anna smirked. He was good. She took a minute to think it through and then replied,

"Are you asking me out on a date?"

"It can be whatever you want it to be, Anna," He replied swiftly.

Anna giggled. She thought about it again. John was so handsome, and he was a manager at an amazing café, but he was way older than her. Was this the right decision? Before Anna could contemplate her decision, she had sent her reply,

"It's a date then, John."

She was excited to see where this would lead.

Chapter 2: First Times

Tall mahogany walls.

Pristine table tops.

Fancy silverware.

Anna had been sitting in the soft, cushioned, and tall chair for about fifteen minutes now. She had ample time to take in her surroundings, and Anna had come to one conclusion.

This was the fanciest place Anna had ever set foot in.

She was trying hard not to let her surprise show in her features. But, every time she caught a glimpse of the embroidered red curtains and gold-tinted windows separating the dining area from the kitchen, her eyebrows touched her hairline. She felt so out of place, but she could also credit that to the fact that this was her first official date.

After agreeing to go out with John, Anna replayed the consequences a hundred times in her head. Throughout high school, she never let herself get caught up in the idea of dating. She was too focused on building her art portfolio for her exhibition. A handful of boys had asked her out, but she rejected them by saying,

"I don't really have the time for dating."

But John wasn't a boy. He was a man. A man who was much older than her and clearly had much more experience in the dating department because of his flirting skills. Anna was a nervous wreck. Her hands were sweaty, and her knees couldn't stop shaking. She had changed her outfit seven times before deciding on the first outfit she had picked. Her room was an absolute disaster. You could define it as a war zone with clothes strewn across the floor and makeup scattered on the dressing table. She kept pulling at her dress, feeling insecure about the length. Was it too short? Too long? She didn't want John to think that she was expecting something out of this date. She wasn't ready to take things further than an innocent dinner in a much too fancy restaurant.

Anna had downed two mint lemonades in the time that she was waiting, so naturally, she had to use the bathroom. It was difficult to navigate through the expansive restaurant floor, and if she wasn't careful, she was sure that she would slip on the smooth wooden panels. Anna kept her eyes trained on the floor, and she couldn't help but notice how shiny it was. She could almost see her reflection on the brown surface, reflecting the ceiling lights back into her eyes. The lights were dizzying, and Anna couldn't shake off the feeling of being misplaced. When John picked the restaurant, she thought it would be a local place she frequented with her friends. She seemed to have forgotten that John was a grown man who probably took multiple women to various fancy restaurants because that is how adults went on dates.

Then her thoughts started to spiral. Was this a bad idea? Should she have chosen such an older man to be her first date? She had zero experience, while he had way too much. Would this date go sideways? Anna found her way to the bathroom; after asking directions from the waiter. She stumbled back to her table, but she stopped in her tracks. It seemed that John had arrived while she was in the bathroom, and he was waiting in the chair across from the one Anna had occupied. She had to take a moment to gather herself before approaching him. Anna took a deep breath and started walking towards him.

"Oh, hey! I saw your purse, but you weren't there. I was starting to think that you ran away," John chuckled as soon as he saw Anna walking towards him.

"Oh, no. I was just in the bathroom. It took me a while to find it. This place is so…big," Anna smiled nervously as she sat herself down at the table. She didn't want to sound as nervous as she felt.

"Yeah. It's one of my favorite restaurants. The food is delicious!" John added with an appreciative smile.

"I…I've never been to a restaurant like this," Anna muttered quietly.

"Well, it's perfect for dates," John mentioned with a soft smile.

"I wouldn't know. I've… I've never been on a date before," Anna admitted reluctantly.

John's smile fell so fast that Anna almost got whiplash.

"What?!" He asked in a ridiculous tone as if it was so hard to believe that this was Anna's first date.

"Um…yeah," Anna smiled sheepishly.

"I…didn't know that. I mean… you just graduated high school, so I thought that maybe you had a boyfriend or two," John explained, taking a tentative sip of his wine.

"Yeah, no. I've never been in a relationship before. Not even a date," Anna said embarrassingly.

This had never bothered her before, but seeing John's reaction made her feel a little small. Was he judging her?

"Well, that's okay. It just kind of changes things. It puts some pressure on me because I don't want your first experience to be bad," he explained softly, brows furrowed.

"Oh, I don't want you to be pressured..." Anna trailed off.

"No. No, don't get me wrong, Anna. I think you're a lovely girl, and I want to get to know you better, especially your work. It's just...I'm not really looking for a serious relationship right now," John explained tentatively.

"Oh, that's okay with me. I've never dated anyone, so I don't think I should rush into anything serious either," Anna explained.

"Well, that's perfect, Anna. I think you and I will have a lot of fun together," John smiled, raising his glass towards Anna.

"I'm looking forward to it, John," Anna smiled back, sighing in relief.

This conversation really took the pressure off. They were just two individuals looking for a good time and nothing serious.

"So, I think it's about time we ordered some food," John suggested, placing his almost empty glass down on the table.

"Hmm, I'll let you decide, seeing how you know this place so well," Anna added with a smile.

"Smart girl," John said suggestively.

Anna couldn't help but blush at that. She tucked her hair behind her ear and giggled as John gestured for the waiter to take their order. Perhaps, this was a good idea after all.

To Anna's disappointment, the date came to an end much too quickly. Time flew by, and before Anna knew it, the two had finished their main course and desert. John was right. The food was absolutely divine. John and Anna spend their time talking about Anna's work. He was so interested in her process and how she got the inspiration to create such unique pieces. Anna remained flattered throughout the date, and she loved talking about her art. She showed John some of the new pieces she was working on, and he was blown away.

"You're an extremely talented girl, Anna. You have a brilliant mind," John spoke softly while they were walking out of the restaurant.

"You're flattering me too much, John," Anna replied shyly.

"Credit where credit is due, Anna," John insisted.

They started walking towards the parking lot, and John spoke up again,

"Allow me to give you a ride back home. It's getting too late for you to take an uber."

Anna thought over the offer, and she realised that it meant that she could spend more time with John, so she said,

"I'd love to, John. Thank you."

The ride back wasn't long, but it was filled with laughter and flirting. John was a very charming man, and he didn't even have to try hard to make Anna blush. He even held Anna's hand and gave it a gentle kiss while he was driving, and Anna swooned. They reached her apartment building much too soon, and Anna had to let go of John's hand, albeit reluctantly.

"I had a wonderful time tonight, John," Anna said with a huge smile, "this was the perfect first date."

"I'm glad you had fun, Anna. I would love to see you again for another date. We can go to a less fancy restaurant this time," John joked.

"I would love to see you again. I'm free next weekend if you would like to meet?" Anna giggled.

"It's a date. Anna," John said with a soft smile.

There was a moment of silence. The two of them were just staring into each other's eyes. Anna had to break the silence,

"Well, thank you again for dropping me back home. Goodnight, John," she smiled as she opened the car door.

"Goodnight, Anna," John whispered.

Anna walked back to her apartment with a ridiculously huge smile on her face. She couldn't wait for next weekend.

That night, Anna slept with butterflies in her stomach and comfort in her heart.

The weekend came in the blink of an eye, and before Anna knew it, she was in an ice cream shop sitting across from John, laughing at a joke he had just made about her picking vanilla.

"It's just such a basic choice, Anna. You could've picked peanut butter or cookies and cream, but vanilla? I'm sorry, but I'm judging you," John laughed.

"Hey, it's not basic! It's a classic," Anna retorted while laughing.

They had been holding hands ever since they sat down, and Anna loved the way he gently stroked her palm with his thumb. Her cheeks hurt from smiling constantly, but she guessed it was a fair price for spending time with a man like John. The last time they had met, they spent the entire time talking about Anna and her work, so Anna wanted to get to know John more on this date.

"So, you own the coffee shop, right? How did that happen?" Anna asked, taking a small bite of her ice cream.

"Well, I was always interested in brewing my own coffee, and when I graduated high school, I realized that college wasn't for me. I stayed with my parents for a year, and they lent me start-up money to start a business. I chose a coffee shop because I knew a lot about brewing coffee, and, well, ten years later, here we are," he chuckled nervously.

"Wow, you say it like it's no big deal. The shop is very successful, John. You should be proud of yourself," Anna smiled, tightening her grip on his hand.

"Well, if you say so, Anna," he smiled gently.

After they finished their ice cream, the two went back to John's car because he insisted on dropping Anna back home again. Who was Anna to refuse his offer? John drove slowly, wanting to spend more time with Anna, and he did not let go of her hand. Soon enough, they were in front of Anna's apartment building again.

"Thank you for seeing me again, Anna. I love spending time with you," John spoke in a hushed tone.

"I love spending time with you too, John," Anna replied.

Silence befell the car once again, and this time, Anna allowed herself to get lost in John's eyes. She felt like she was drowning, but she could not bring herself to look away. She inched closer, but she stopped once she realized what she was aiming for.

"Are…are you okay with this, Anna?" John asked quietly, understanding what was happening.

"I…" Anna took a sharp breath.

She had never done this before, but she wanted to take this step with John. She knew that he would make her feel good.

"Yes, John. I want to," she whispered into the small distance between their lips.

That was all John needed, and he placed a firm hand on Anna's face, inching her closer.

Anna's heart had never beat this fast, and she thought it would jump out of her chest. She closed her eyes slightly as she felt John's lips ghost over hers. He was breathing slowly, and Anna felt goosebumps rise all over her arms when his lips slightly touched hers. It was like he was asking for permission once again, so as a response, Anna closed the distance between them. Then she felt fireworks. John's lips were soft and gentle, and Anna gasped when he slightly inched his tongue into her mouth. She felt warm all over, and she fell into John, letting him deepen the kiss.

It was safe to say that her first kiss was nothing short of magical.

Chapter 3: Here and There

Anna replayed her first kiss in her head over and over again. She felt the tenderness of John's lips each time she did so.

It was magical.

She wanted more. But it was the last time she saw John. He hadn't met her, talked to her, or even so much as dropped a text since.

"Does he still like me?" she wondered to herself. It was a bit peculiar of John not to reach out to her after that perfect kiss. He knew she was interested in him, and she was pretty sure he liked her just as much.

"Maybe it wasn't as special to John as it was for me," she questioned herself." He's much older with far greater romantic experience; maybe I wasn't even in his top five kisses. Do I ask him what went wrong? Am I overthinking this? Of course, he'd call; he said he 'loved' spending time with me; that must mean something, right? He'll come around; he must be busy with the coffee shop. I'm not going to drive myself crazy thinking about this. We agreed this was casual".

She had to stop her trail of thought as a notification popped on her laptop screen from her art school. She had applied to the best art school in her state. She wasn't really planning to go to college, but her motivation came from the last time she met John. She thought he was so mesmerized by her art; if she got in, he'd be really proud.

Much to her excitement, she was offered a scholarship for her program. "They must've really liked my artwork; after all, John called me talented and brilliant, he has a flair for the finer things in life, like aesthetics and art, so coming from him, it means something," she decided.

Anna had gotten a job at a cafe near her campus. She wanted to ask John for work but didn't want to come off too strong. She trained to be a barista so that the next time they met, she would finally have something in common with him.

"I'm gonna blow him away with my skills, he'd point out something I'm doing wrong, jokingly, and we will have a big laugh about it," she anticipated in joy.

A whole month went by.

Anna had almost given up hope on her budding romance with her attractive boyfriend, constantly thinking about what she did wrong when she received a DM on her Instagram.

It was John!

"Can't stop thinking about you, Anna, it's so unlike me, but this is how you make me feel. You're just remarkable. I can't wait to see more of your artistic creations. When can I see you again?"

Anna was smiling ear to ear as she read the words on her phone screen. "I knew it wasn't over," she whispered, relieved.

Anna invited John to the cafe at her campus. It was a small, cozy place but highlighted artwork from all of the school's best artists. Anna was one of them. She pointed out her painting on the brick wall.

"That's mine," she said giddily.

"You blow my mind, Anna; I can't believe I get to know someone so talented as you. And with the scholarship, your folks must be proud", he said.

Anna couldn't hide the glee she felt inside. John had that effect on her; like warm soup on a cold winter night, she felt at home when she was with him.

"Wait till you see my latte skills" she quickly went behind the counter to make him a cup. She drew a heart with the milk foam as she poured over the steamed milk on the freshly brewed espresso.

"Is that supposed to be a heart, it kind of looks like a bird," John let out a giggle. Anna laughed back.

"Hey! I drew a heart on coffee for you; just appreciate that".

"I do, I do; it's just that I'm not a fan of latte; I'm more of an Americano guy. But I would drink this for you." John walked up to her, grabbed the cup, and put it to his lips. Anna wanted to kiss those lips.

She looked at him with hopeful eyes, and he wiped some of the foam from his cup and put it on Anna's nose.

"You're a dork; you know that, right? He grabbed her by the waist, pulled her close, and kissed her. At that moment, Anna felt like everything around her had disappeared, it was just her and John, and nothing else existed. Not the brick walls of the cafe nor the campus, there was just a collision of her and him, and there was stardust all around.

She ran her fingers through his hair and said, "Your eyes are so dreamy. Did anyone tell you that?

"Yes, I've heard that compliment many, many times," John laughed.

"I feel like I've known you my whole life, and it's only been a couple of months. There's just this chemistry between us". She admitted to him.

"It's undeniable," John went on, "You've made quite an impression on me."

"I just feel so safe around you, John, like I can tell you anything like I feel like I can trust you," Anna said.

John looked at her, taken aback by these words; he grabbed her chin and kissed her again.

They walked the campus the entire evening, holding hands and sharing a bagel. Anna told him about her new friends on the campus, took him to the halls, and showed him some more paintings she was working on. John seemed genuinely interested in them. He spoke so enthusiastically about each and every one of them. Anna noticed how her fingers fit perfectly into John's. He was so handsome and rugged. She couldn't believe he was with her. It was like her own perfect meet cute.

The next day she went to meet her friends at a taco shack.

"You guys, he's just so *perfect,* I can't believe I get to be with him," she exclaimed.

"He really is the perfect man, so gentle and polite, also the best boss," her friend who worked at John's café said." I'm so jealous of you."

"I'm a lucky girl," Anna agreed as she gobbled on her taco.

"When he talks about my art, I feel like my artwork comes to life." Anna and John went on a few more dates in the coming weeks. He took her on a boat ride, and they saw fireworks while holding onto each other.

Then they went biking in the park. John showed her the best picnic spots to watch the sunset from. They saw the sun go down in each other's arms. Anna had grown so familiar with the shape of John's face, the texture of his hair, his perfect jawline, the curve of his smile, and how her hand fit into hers. She felt like she had found the one. She caught herself humming to the songs he shared with her.

He was always on her mind. Anna woke up one morning; she held up her brush to her blank canvas and started painting.

She picked each color from the palette and blended it onto the canvas and it started to form a picture. As one color melted into another, it became a memory that came to life. It was the sunset that John showed her at the park, from their spot. It was her and him, holding each other as if nothing could ever go wrong.

A warm feeling overcame Anna, she took a picture of the painting from her phone and sent it to John. She knew he would love it. She found herself smiling at the thought of him analyzing the painting.

Anna knew then that what she felt was real. As real as the brush in her hands, as real as the white fabric of the canvas before her, as real as the dusky sunset she had painted over it. She knew it was the *real deal.* She was in love with her perfect man. She couldn't wait to tell her friends. She couldn't wait to tell him. Her heart paced in excitement. She felt tethered to John. Like an invisible string always pulled her close to him. She yearned for his presence when she was alone. His arms around her, felt like home. Her sanctuary, he completed her.

John swiped his phone to see the picture Anna had sent him. It was a painting she had made, it seemed familiar. He examined it closely and realized it was a scene from their date at the park.

The breathtaking sunset. He remembered how happy Anna looked when he took her to that spot. She was beaming. He thought to himself,

"She is truly gifted, to recreate such a beautiful memory, so perfectly, with just a canvas and a brush. I must've made an impact on her that day that she remembers it all so vividly. She must really be interested in spending time with me. I can see it all in her eyes, how they inspect my face when I'm with her, how they get lost in my eyes." And then it dawned on him.

"Anna must be in love with me."

Chapter 4: Secret Tales of a Drunk

Evening classes.

The early morning bird songs.

The smell of fresh brewing coffee.

The ding of the cash register.

A heavy heart.

Anna closed the lid on her fifth cappuccino of the morning. She wanted to chug the disposable cup down in one go to gain strength to get through the day. Her eyes were slowly shutting from the weight of an unfinished sleep cycle.

Her fingers permanently smelled like a weird mixture of stale coffee and dried-out acrylics. Anna's days consisted of waking up at the crack of dawn, taking a cold shower to jolt herself awake, slipping on any clothes that seemed clean, and rushing to open the coffee shop. She cleaned the tables and started up the espresso machine.

By 7 am, Anna was greeting a line of sleep-deprived and overworked college students who were desperate for their daily dose of caffeine.

Anna's shift ended by noon and she had to rush to campus to attend hours of classes with no breaks in between. She barely had time to stuff a sandwich in her mouth so as to not collapse on the campus grounds. By 6 pm, Anna stumbled out of her studio class with her canvases tucked tightly under her arms and a cramp in her wrist that seemed to make a permanent home there. She dragged her feet back to her apartment and collapsed on her sofa, passing out as soon as her head hit the cushions. She would jolt awake to her blaring alarm much too soon, starting the exhausting day all over again.

All of her days blended together in a blurry haze of exhaustion and the pungent scent of coffee. Perhaps it was good that Anna didn't have time to breathe. That meant she didn't have time to think. And that meant that she didn't think of *him*. She didn't think of how he gave her a taste of safety, hope, kindness, and love. She didn't think of how he snatched it all away from her in the blink of an eye, leaving her lost. Confused. Abandoned.

Anna didn't think of how it had been a year. It had been a year since she had seen John. A year since she touched his soft face with the tip of her fingers. A year since she felt his warm breath on her starting lips. But he still managed to creep into her mind during the day. It happened so suddenly. Almost like a silent attack.

Slowly.

He crept back into her mind, nestling in the corner and growing bigger until Anna felt tears falling down her cheeks.

Every time she thought that she finally had him, he pushed her away. He left her blindsided. She thought that they would be beautiful together, but he proved her wrong time and time again. She was left craving his touch. He left her whenever he pleased. Anna could not let him go. John took her first kiss from her, and from that moment, Anna had given herself to him.

Anna was an empty shell at this point. She didn't get it. John was the one who pursued her. He asked her out first. He kissed her. Why would he ghost her like this? Was he unsure of his feelings for her? He told her that he wasn't looking for anything serious, but did that mean that he would stop talking to her for a year? Not even a few weeks or months. A whole year. Did he find someone else? Had he replaced Anna? After she made that painting for him, she thought that he would realize that they were more than just a fling. Anna poured her feelings into that painting. She wanted to burn it to ashes so she wouldn't be reminded of how naïve she had been. Why would an older and experienced man like John fall for a college student like Anna?

"Did you get any sleep?"

The question pulled Anna out of her spiraling thoughts.

She looked up from her sketchbook and saw one of her friends pulling out the chair in front of Anna and taking a seat on the café's table. It was almost noon, so the morning rush had died down, and Anna had taken a small break to work on one of her assignments.

"Enough to not faint in the middle of class, but that's not enough," Anna quipped dryly.

Her friend slid a sandwich in her direction and gave her a sympathetic smile.

"Eat something, Anna. You need it," she said quietly.

Anna didn't argue with that because she felt the knots in her stomach tighten. She unwrapped the sandwich with shaky fingers and bit into the soft bread. She hadn't realized how hungry she was, so she scarfed it down in a rushed manner and took a big gulp of her iced coffee. She felt a little more awake.

"You need to take care of yourself, Anna. You're overworking yourself. This isn't healthy," her friend advised with furrowed brows.

"I like being busy. It means I can't think about..." she trailed off because saying his name was too painful.

"John?" her friend finished it for her.

She hadn't heard the name in so long that it seemed unfamiliar. But the sting was still fresh and Anna couldn't help the wince that showed on her face.

"I don't want to think about him," she said in a resolute manner, but her friend saw through it.

"But he's still consuming you, Anna. You can't just avoid him and your feelings. Let yourself feel hurt," her friend said earnestly.

"I can't. It's too much," Anna said in a pained voice.

She got up from her table to avoid her friend's words. She started cleaning up because it was time to close up the café and rush to class. Anna was tempted to skip her classes today and take a long well-deserved nap. She started wiping the counter and shutting off the espresso machine when she felt her phone buzzing in her back pocket. She was tempted to ignore it, but it kept vibrating so she slipped it out and looked at the screen.

Her eyes widened when she saw the call.

Incoming call from John

Anna blinked twice, expecting herself to be hallucinating.

But this was actually happening. John was calling her.

Anna had not seen his name on her phone screen for a whole year.

She had to pick up.

It was like an automatic response. She swiped her screen and put the phone to her ear. She kept quiet, still in disbelief at what was happening. Then she heard his voice.

It was slurred.

He was mumbling and Anna heard his labored breaths.

He sounded drunk.

Then Anna heard the first coherent word her spoke since she had picked up the call,

"A…n…Anna?"

Anna found herself on a bus. How did she get here? It was like her body was functioning on autopilot. After she heard John say her name in a slurred tone, she realized that he was very drunk. She asked him,

"John? Are you okay?"

"No…I need you. Please come to me. I need you," John mumbled into the phone.

Anna heard a crash, and she rushed out of the café, telling her friend to lock up. Her friend was left there shocked and confused, but Anna didn't have time to explain.

She asked John to send her his location, and he was about a thirty-minute bus ride from campus. The ride was excruciating for Anna because she was worried that John would hurt himself. Why was he so drunk? Why did he call Anna and say that he needed her? He hadn't reached out in a year. Why, all of a sudden, did he think of Anna?

Anna knew that she was giving in too easily. She shouldn't be rushing to him at one call. He left her in pieces. Why was Anna rushing to him?

Because I love him.

She told herself. Like a fool. She was still in love with him.

The bus stopped after what felt like hours and Anna jumped out onto the pavement. She followed the location on her phone and her feet stopped in front of a very sketchy and isolated motel.

This didn't feel like a good idea.

The motel sign was flickering, and Anna could see the mold in the walls as she stepped into the motel's lot. She saw a few people clammer into their rooms. She could smell the liquor and she wrapped her arms around herself and rushed to the room that John was in. he was in room 302. Anna found it after rushing past two men who were drinking outside their rooms, staring at her as she walked by. Anna took a deep breath and contemplated her actions once again. Before she could talk herself out of it, she knocked.

She heard crashes from inside the room and the door thumped before she heard the lock unlatch. The white door, with paint peeling off the corners, creaked open, and Anna finally saw him. After a year, she looked at john's face. She couldn't recognize him. his hair was a disheveled mess. His eyes were red and swollen like he had been crying.

"You came," he croaked, and Anna could smell the liquor on his breath.

He stepped back, inviting her in, and Anna stepped on the dirty red motel room's carpet. She cast her gaze across the room, which was an absolute mess. The bed was unmade and the sheets were jumbled up on the floor. She saw cigarette butts and ash strewn across the table and the carpet. One of the lamps had fallen on the floor, and Anna assumed that was the crash she heard on the phone.

"John…what happened? What are you doing here?" Anna asked, sitting on the dresser's chair.

John locked the door and stumbled onto the bed, falling face-first into the pillow.

He mumbled something, but Anna couldn't catch it.

"What?" She asked in a soft voice.

He looked up. his face was red from the drinks he had, and he whispered,

"I miss you."

Anna's breath was caught in her throat. Her heart started beating fast, but she kept her cool.

"You haven't talked to me in a year, John. Why did you call me out of the blue?"

"I never stopped thinking about you, Anna," he said with soft eyes.

"Why did you leave me then, John?" She asked in a stern tone, but her voice was breaking.

"It's…it's complicated, Anna. I haven't been fully honest with you. I thought this would be a fling, but my feelings for you are different. I've never felt this before," he explained in a broken voice.

"What have you not been honest about?" Anna asked with furrowed brows.

"You will never look at me the same," John explained, looking down at the carpeted floor.

"John…I can't stop thinking about you. This year was the toughest year of my life. I can't just forget about you. Tell me. Please," Anna pleaded in a whispered tone.

"I…I'm married, Anna," John said in a quiet voice that broke off into a sob.

At that moment, Anna's whole world fell apart.

Chapter 5: Forgive and Forget

"*Anna? Anna! Would you please say something?*", John begged as he shook Anna who was completely dumbfounded. She jolted out of her trance and stared into John's light brown eyes with inexplicable pain.

She opened her mouth to say something, but no words came out. For once in her life, she truly was gobsmacked. She felt betrayed, she felt cheated on, she felt lost but most of all she felt like she was sinking in a huge pool of quicksand, with a heavy weight dangling around her neck. She wanted to get out of that place, she wanted to run away from John as far as possible.

John tried to hug her, but his voice was nearly gone, *"Please Anna, listen to me, just hear me out…,"* he grabbed her hand lovingly and kissed it.

But she pulled away from him, a fat tear rolled down her left cheek as she slammed the door in John's face.

Anna woke up to the buzzing of her alarm, she annoyingly snoozed it. It was *finals week.* She just wanted to stay in bed, she never wanted to get out of her warm bed again. It was her only source of comfort. She missed *him* too much.

Then she suddenly saw John's Iron Maiden hoodie lying on the armchair across her room. Her heart started to race. He had given it to her on a date when they went cycling at the park and she had felt cold from the breeze. She immediately got up and put it on and climbed back in bed. It smelled like him.

It was the only thing she had left of him.

She missed his cologne, his soothing embrace, his tousled hair, the scruff of his beard when it rubbed against her soft face, his tender lips, and his gentle kisses that made everything around her disappear. She longed to be back in his arms but instead, felt a sinking feeling in the pit of her stomach.

"He's married…"

She started to sob uncontrollably.

Anna tossed and turned in her bed for another hour, her pillowcase was now drenched in tears. She just loved him so intensely. How would she live without him?

All Anna wanted to do was lie in her quilt in a fetal position for the rest of her day. She stared at the half-finished painting from last week's assignment, on the canvas next to her bed. Anna had zero motivation to complete it. It was a desert sunset. She thought to herself,

"Another sunset. So ironic that now, the sun has set on John and me…it's not fair, I do not deserve this pain" as she felt a painful lump in her throat and wept in despair. Her stomach growled but she ignored it, buried her head inside the sheets, switched her phone off, and went back to sleep.

There was a loud bang on the door, Anna rubbed her eyes and asked groggily, *"Who is it?"*. It was her friend, Liz, "Where were you, yesterday? she asked. "You missed the sculpturing exam, you didn't show up to work either, I had to cover your shift, the cafe was flooding, I was swamped till 10 last night. Anna, what's wrong? Are you still thinking about *him?"*

"No…", Anna lied and frowned at her friend.

"Please Anna, look at yourself, when was the last time you showered, did you eat anything at all? You look like you're starving. Don't you get it? He's no good for you! You need to get out of this bipolar relationship", she replied with worry in her voice.

Anna shook her head and buried her face in the palms of her hands.

"Let's get something to eat, let's go have blueberry pancakes at the diner, c'mon now, get up, get yourself cleaned up, I'll meet you in the lobby downstairs", Liz said, as she left Anna moping in her bed.

The next week was a blur, Anna managed to get to work and sat for her printmaking exam too, but her painting back home was still waiting for her to complete it.

She constantly got flashbacks of John, his words, his smile, all she could think of, was *him,* his voice was stuck in her head, but she tried to disregard her train of thought by picking up extra chores at the cafe.

She was scrubbing the countertop when Luke from Kappa Pi, walked in, holding brightly colored flyers in his hands. "There's a party at our frat house tonight, Anna, you should come", handing her a flyer and pinning another to the bulletin board on the wall of the cafe.

Anna decided to dress up and go to the party. She thought a loud, social event might get her into a different state of mind, but she was wrong.

All her friends were dancing, chugging beer, doing headstands, and playing beer pong while she crept away to the patio and stared at the night sky.

Her heart incessantly pined for John. She just felt out of place. Anna wanted to crawl back into her bed and look at their pictures together. But she had promised her friends she'd stay and have fun. Her friends were busy getting into antics and hooking up with guys while she wandered on the patio alone.

She was making her way toward the kitchen to refill her drink when two guys in togas grabbed her and threw her into the pool. Before she could conceive what had happened, her bag started to vibrate, she frantically managed to get herself out of the pool, dried her hands, and checked to see who was calling.

There it was. John's name is on the screen. She thought she'd never hear his voice again. Her heart raced in anticipation. She impulsively walked out of the party, away from the loud music and the commotion, and into the quiet street pacing her way back into her dorm. It was still ringing. She was torn between missing him and feeling betrayed. Her hands were shaking. She swiped to answer.

"Anna? I was hoping you'd answer. How have you been?", he asked in a mellow voice.

All memories of John came back rushing to Anna's head, but she kept her calm and answered politely, "I am okay, John, how are you?"

"I am better now, but that night, everything that went down, I just wanted to apologize. For being drunk. For hiding the fact that I am married. *For everything*", John said in a shaky voice. He went on "I just want you to know how truly sorry I am, Anna…"

Anna started tearing up, "You broke my heart John, I trusted you, how could you?", she whimpered.

"I didn't want to lose you Anna, when we met, I just, I don't know, you bring out this side of me, I just felt like I want to be around you, so I kept *it* a secret", John admitted, "I still don't want to lose you…"

Anna listened intently.

"But there are things that complicate our situation, so…, I was thinking, it would be better if we just stayed friends".

There was silence. Anna felt dejected. She didn't want to be friends. She wanted more. But if being friends meant she would still have John in her life, then, she was open to that idea.

"Anna? Are you still there? Please, just tell me that you forgive me, I need to hear it from you", John breathed heavily.

"Yes, Okay, John, *we can be friends*", Anna said reluctantly, choking on her words. "I forgive you", she added in a low hum.

"I'm so relieved to hear that, you know you mean so much to me Anna, I've got to go now, but I'll see you soon, okay?", John said excitedly.

"Sure", Anna agreed, holding back her tears.

Over the next few months, Anna and John would talk over the phone, frequently. He would often appear in her Instagram DMs and Anna's eyes would light up.

Anna was gradually returning to her routine. She stopped skipping classes and handed in her assignments on time. She even finished her painting of the sunset in the desert. She was cheerful at work, making new friends and learning new skills at the café. Her boss even promised her a promotion looking at how hard she had been working for the past few months.

It seemed like in her mind, John was the source of her happiness and as long as he was there in her life, to talk to, to hold on to, even if it were only a couple of times a month, even if they were *just friends,* it made her really happy. She was not oblivious to the fact that the mere presence of John regulated her psychological well-being.

Anna's friends noticed it too, but to them, it was cause for concern, because they noticed a pattern in John's behavior, he kept entering and exiting Anna's life, they did not appreciate their friend being manipulated like that, and they verbalized their concerns to Anna, but much to their dismay, Anna repeatedly, shrugged them off.

Throughout summer, Anna and John had met quite a few times, he would take her out for lunch, and they would spend the entire evening talking about their childhood, their interests, their fears, and their goals for the future.

By now, they knew each other quite well. They knew about each other's likes and dislikes, and they could tell when one of them was a bit under the weather and knew exactly what to do to comfort and uplift the other.

They would go out to the beach, chase each other around, playfully, or they would drive around in John's car to all the places Anna always wanted to see. Anna was becoming John's weakness. He missed her whenever they were apart, and he especially looked forward to their *friend dates* each week.

But it was not that simple. He could not lead her on and break her heart. She mattered too much.

To Anna, John was like a limb, an extension of her existence, with him, everything made sense, and without him, nothing did.

She felt like an invisible string pulled them toward each other. In her heart, she knew that they were soulmates. That sooner or later, they would somehow end up being together.

But it was the wait, that was killing her. It was eating her from the inside. She tried to conceal her feelings for him, from him, but somehow, they always peeked through. Each time she touched him or hugged him, she wanted more.

Anna didn't know how long she would be able to continue this charade, the thought that he was with someone else just shattered her, that he was holding someone else, kissing someone else, cuddling and sleeping with someone else. It was excruciating to even think of John with another woman.

She just wanted to confront him, and come clean but she was terrified of how he would react. Would he reciprocate her feelings, or would he abandon her completely?

She could not afford to lose John again. It would destroy her.

Chapter 6: Is this Love?

Anna sat impatiently with her phone clasped tightly in her hands. Her leg was shaking, jumping up and down unconsciously.

2 weeks

It had been 2 weeks since she had heard anything from John. No text. No calls. It was like they had reverted back to their old ways.

Regressed.

It was so disappointing.

All those memories they made over the summer played on repeat in Anna's head, filling her with a sense of loss and melancholy.

Had John's marriage caught up to him? Had he forgotten about Anna, choosing his wife over her? Was Anna losing the love of her life all over again?

She was so afraid.

For a moment, she had John in the palm of her hands, close to her heart.

But now, she felt like she had squeezed too tightly, and he was slipping out, leaving her with just memories. Even if they had not defined their relationship as anything more than friends, John had become such a huge part of her life.

She couldn't get a taste of his presence and then forget about him so easily.

Just as Anna's thoughts raced into a spiral, she heard the ding of her phone, which was still clutched tightly in her hands.

The vibrations sent a jolt up her arm, and she almost flinched at the movement. Then she realized that she had just gotten a message.

It was John.

Her heart swelled in her chest. She almost cheered out loud because John was still there. He was still thinking about her. She swiped her phone to open the text, and her face fell again.

"Can I come over? We need to talk," John's text flashed on her screen.

That's never a good sign. Had something happened? Did his wife find out that he was seeing Anna? Anna gulped loudly, and her brows furrowed as she hovered her trembling fingers over the keypad of her phone.

A part of her would not have hesitated a second before telling John to come over, but the other part was apprehensive about what he wanted to discuss.

Would he tell her that they had to stop seeing each other? That would crush Anna. She still wanted to know what was happening, so she texted him back,

"Yeah, sure."

"Okay. Reaching in 20," he replied immediately.

The 20-minute wait was excruciating.

Anna imagined the worst scenarios until her entire body was left trembling. She had to calm herself down by taking a few deep breaths.

Then she heard the bell.

The loud sound echoed off her apartment walls, and she stopped breathing. She dragged her feet to the front door, opening it slowly like she was afraid of what would happen once she let John inside. Then she saw him. he was standing at her door, with his shoulders hunched over and his hands stuffed deep in his hoodie's pockets.

He gave her a slight smile.

"Hey, Anna. I'm sorry for not talking to you for so long. A lot happened," he explained with sad eyes.

Anna stepped aside, gesturing for him to come in.

"What's wrong? Are you okay? I was really worried," Anna said, noticing the redness in John's eyes and the faint scent of alcohol on his breath.

"Umm…I don't know if I'm okay. I…I just got divorced," he announced plainly, taking a seat on Anna's living room couch.

Anna stopped in her tracks. It was like her feet were blocks of ice.

"What? How…" she couldn't finish her sentence.

"I know…it's a lot. I was finalizing everything over the past few weeks. That's why I couldn't talk to or meet you," John explained, smiling softly.

"John…I…I don't know what to say. Does this mean…?" Anna hinted at the question.

"Yes, Anna. We can be together now. Finally, You and me," John sighed with a huge smile.

Anna was out of words. It was like her tongue had knots, so she did what she could only do at that moment. She lurched towards John on the couch, throwing her arms around his neck and straddling him in the process. She hugged him as tightly as she could and burrowed her face in his neck.

"Oh, John! I'm so happy. I missed you so much. I need you," Anna confessed, trying to hold in her excitement.

"I need you too, Anna. I…I love you," John whispered, pulling back and holding Anna's face with both of his hands.

She stared deeply into his eyes, trying not to get lost.

"I love you too, John,' she whispered, leaning in to kiss him passionately.

John's hands found her waist, tightening his grip and pushing her closer to him. the friction elicited a soft moan from Anna's lips, and John took the opportunity to deepen the kiss with his tongue.

Anna's senses were overwhelmed by John, and she let herself drown in his touch. Everywhere his hands traveled, Anna felt electricity travel throughout her body.

He slipped his hands under her shirt, lightly scratching the skin, and Anna almost fainted at the feeling. It was intoxicating.

"Can we…move to the bed?" John asked in a quiet voice.

"I…yes. Yes, John," Anna hesitated at first, but she didn't want the feeling of intoxication to stop.

He smiled widely at her and swooped her up in his arms. He stood up with Anna's legs tightly wrapped around his waist and started venturing into the bedroom. He stumbled a little, and the two laughed at the silliness, but Anna felt at home in his arms.

"It's on the right," Anna giggled, kissing John's neck slowly.

"You're distracting me," he laughed as he finally found his way to Anna's bedroom.

He three Anna on the bed and climbed on top of her, the space between their bodies almost diminishing. Anna gasped, and John slipped off his shirt.

"I've been waiting so long to do this," he said, kissing Anna again.

"Me too," Anna gasped, letting John take control.

That night, Anna's body experienced things it had never before. She felt like she was on fire, but she welcomed the burn.

After so long, Anna and John were finally one.

Winter came around, and the crisp breeze of February evening air struck Anna's cheek.

With the start of winter also came the celebratory anticipation of Valentine's Day.

This was the first time in her life that Anna actually had something to look forward to for the holiday. John and Anna had been spending so much time together, and Anna had never been happy.

He even surprised her by picking her up for a fancy Valentine's Day dinner date. Anna had put on in a stunning red dress that had been catching dust at the back of her closet, and she felt beautiful.

John made her feel beautiful.

The car ride to the restaurant was filled with sweet exchanges,

"You look beautiful."

"I missed you."

"I love you."

Anna's cheeks were as red as her dress by the time they reached the restaurant.

John didn't let go of her hand until they were seated at their table. It took Anna a moment to notice how fancy the restaurant was. John has an eye for elegant places, and Anna was getting used to being spoiled. John treated her like a princess, and she reveled in it.

"We'll have your finest bottle of wine," John ordered the waiter with a huge smile.

He was simply glowing, and it brought a smile to Anna's face.

"You need to stop spoiling me, John," Anna chuckled, taking his hand in hers once again.

"Never, my love," he replied, placing a gentle kiss on her knuckles.

Anna felt like she was on top of the world.

But something in the back of her mind was coming in the way of her happiness. Ever since John told her about his divorce, Anna felt like something was wrong.

He had been too casual in his announcement, and he showed no sign of remorse or loss. She knew that he wasn't happy in his marriage, but he still had a wife. They were partners for years.

How could he so easily disregard his marriage as if it never existed?

Did he really get divorced, or did he just say that so Anna would agree to be with him?

Anna's intrusive thoughts were eating away at her happiness, but she didn't want to bring it up with John because it sounded like she was accusing him.

She wanted to trust the man she had given her heart to, but it was getting more difficult as time progressed.

He always changed the topic when Anna asked him how or why he got the divorce. He didn't even tell Anna how his wife reacted.

It was all a bit suspicious.

"What are you thinking about, Anna?" John's voice brought her out of her thoughts.

"Oh, nothing. I'm…I'm just really happy to be here with you, John," Anna replied, squeezing his hand tightly.

"I'm really happy too, Anna," John said.

That's when the wine and food arrived, so Anna decided to drown her worries in the red liquid and let John enter her heart, mind, and body.

Anna was at the starting point once again.

She had been texting John constantly for the past three days, and he had not responded.

It was scaring her because it was so unlike him.

He always responded to Anna, so this was very uncharacteristic of him. Had something happened? Was he hurt? Was his wife back? Anna couldn't help but reach insane conclusions.

She was afraid that something bad had happened to John. She couldn't lose him.

That's when her phone rang.

She jumped to grab it off her bed, hoping to see John's name pop up on the screen. But her smile fell when she saw it was a call from an unknown number. She started at it for a few minutes, unable to register the call. Then she snapped herself out of it and picked it up.

Anna heard static on the other line.

There was silence, and then she heard the cracked voice,

"Hello, is this Anna?"

Anna blinked a few times at the strange occurrence.

"Um…yes," she responded.

"We are calling you with the concern of our patient, John. You were on his emergency contacts list," they explained.

Anna's heart fell to the floor. All of her intrusive thoughts had proven themselves to be right.

"What happened to John? Is he okay?" Anna asked fervently.

"We are calling from the rehab center he was just admitted to. We were asked to inform you that John will not be in contact for some time because he will be here," they explained.

At that moment, Anna's world came crashing down once again.

Every time she took one step closer to John, he was taken three steps away.

Chapter 7: Therapy

*T*ick tock. Tick tock. Tick tock. Tick tock.

The grandfather clock in the waiting area chimed 4 o'clock.

Anna clasped her fingers together tightly. She proceeded to pick the skin on her knuckles nervously. She looked around the room, people were busy on their phones or reading a magazine. She ran her fingers through her hair and adjusted her posture. Anna had come for her therapist's appointment.

As she waited for her turn, she thought about the events that had transpired over the last few months. John had been admitted to rehab, Anna felt so betrayed by this.

How could he do this to me?

She thought to herself.

He promised he would change. I am such a fool. I trick myself into trusting him over and over again. He must be feeling so devastated after his divorce, he must be missing her, that's why he's drinking again! And taking oxycodone! It must be to escape the pain he's in. That's so unlike John. Does that mean he still loves her?

Anna was spiraling. She had been doing this for the past two months. She had barely gotten any sleep and her dark under eyes were a telltale sign. She had distanced herself from her friends, choosing not to reply to their texts and downright ignoring their calls. Anna had lost her appetite and even the sight of food made her uneasy. All she did was stay in her bed for as long as possible since it was the only thing that gave her some sense of comfort and warmth.

The reason she was at her therapist's office was because she had been having a series of panic attacks, each time she left her room to go out in public. She would stop midway of performing simple tasks such as going to class or working her shift at the café. She would have these heart palpitations that would make her feel her heart would literally burst out of her chest, but she promised herself she wouldn't tell a soul and figure it out all on her own.

A petite, blonde woman emerged from the hallway and announced nonchalantly, "Ms. Anna, Dr. Zara will see you now".

Anna timidly stepped into Dr. Zara's office. It was a dimly lit room with gold sconces over solid khaki wallpaper. On one side of the room, was an Amazonian green velvet couch flanked by two beige couches with gold accents.

A large chevron patterned rug adorned the sleek hardwood flooring. The other side of the room was covered by a ginormous ficus. The largest Anna had ever seen. Next to it was a wall mounted bookcase and a painting of a zebra grazing in what seemed like the African savanna as the sun set in the background.

The ficus casted a shadow on the birchwood center table that had an assorted display of a tissue box, a leather notebook embossed with the initials Z.A, a fountain pen, a tiny vase with chrysanthemums and a lit candle that smelled like vanilla and cinnamon.

Anna took it all in as she sighed and sat down on the green couch and Dr. Zara sat next to her on the beige one.

Dr. Zara Ivanov was a doctor of psychiatry, a graduate of Yale and in her mid-thirties. She had a poised demeanor about her as she inspected Anna with her hazel brown eyes. Her polished auburn waves rested on one side of her slender neck. She ardently asked, "Hello Anna, so nice to meet you, how are you today?"

Anna composed her wayward thoughts and answered, "I've been better" and managed a weary smile.

"If you're ready and relaxed, we can start the session", Zara inquired, to which Anna nodded and she continued, "So, what seems to be bothering you?"

Anna recapped the events of the past year and focused on her deteriorating mental health over the past two months. She told Zara about the nuances of her relationship with John, the time she spent with him, the bond they formed over that time and the betrayal she felt when he told her he was married. Pausing to break down in tears as Zara comforted her with tissues. She explained to Zara how John had a pattern of entering and exiting her life at his will and how this last time, she thought, when John told her he was divorced, and they made love, she knew he was in for the long run.

Zara listened to Anna intently and scribbled in her leather notebook as Anna poured her heart out.

"Then I got a call from the rehab center", Anna sniffled, "they told me he was staying with them; he had been taking oxycodone and he was so drunk he crashed into parked car", she hid her face behind the palms of her hands.

"I thought we shared everything, I didn't know he was carrying so much pain, I feel so blindsided, so betrayed, I trusted him, he told me he was past his old habits, he was over *her…*", Anna broke into tears again.

It was grueling for Anna to put her feelings into words. She felt so vulnerable, so naked, in front of Zara. Her heart ached for John, she hadn't heard from him in so long, she longed to hear his voice, feel his touch, the grief overcame her like a dark cloud as she felt completely lost.

Zara listened to Anna's heartbreak with undivided attention. "Anna, why do you think John left you in the dark about his marriage?", she asked.

"He wanted to protect me, he had fallen in love with me, and this was the only way that we could be together", Anna exclaimed.

"Let's view this from a different vantage point, can you consider the possibility that John might have been manipulating you to satisfy his needs?", Zara asked unperturbedly.

Anna looked at her in disbelief. She didn't want to hear any of it. She just wanted to crawl back into the security of her bed.

"I have a class in less than an hour", she took a big gulp of water, "Can we continue this later?", she asked.

Zara replied, "Of course, but I have some homework for you, you must write down a list of reasons as to why John might not be the right person for you, we will discuss that in the next session", she said closing her notebook.

Anna felt horrible as she left Zara's office. She felt as if Zara preyed on her insecurities. She had come to Zara seeking help for her panic attacks, instead Zara had made John look like the villain in Anna's eyes when he himself had been in so much pain.

Over the course of the next month, the sessions with Zara continued, Anna would comply with the home assignments and show up each time, but each time she left Zara's office feeling worse than before she came.

Anna simply did not want John out of her life. She still had the glimmering hope than John would make amends with her and return to her life, never to leave again. However, Zara insisted that Anna was chasing a mirage. John would do no such thing. She affirmed that he had never been upfront with Anna and toyed with her emotions to satiate himself.

Zara persisted that Anna should practice self-love, that she should look beyond this relationship and realize that she has her whole life ahead of her. She should make herself her primary focus. Do things that made her happy. Like creating art. Focus on her schoolwork and the rest of the relationships in her life.

Anna, on the other hand, turned a heedless ear to Zara's advice. She burrowed herself deeper into her longing for John. Fantasizing of what they *could have* been together, instead of what they actually were.

She found herself often dissociating from reality and forgetting what she was doing. She got lost on campus grounds multiple times, the same grounds that were home to her, struggling to find her way back to her dorm.

Her friends were furious of how Anna had let herself go, they wanted to comfort her, be there for her but she would only push them farther away. She would miss her classes and just wander around the campus in misery. She had lost quite a bit of weight; all her clothes were too big for her now. It was because she went days without food, surviving on only coffee or the occasional bag of chips if she felt like she would collapse in public.

Anna's grades took a nosedive, and her university was concerned if she would be able to retain her art scholarship. She was called to the dean's office and given the warning.

This was the blow that Anna needed to wake up from the fever dream she had been living in for so long.

Anna decided she would try to crawl out of this hole of despair, that she had dug for herself. She would try to distract herself to shut her gloomy thoughts down.

Anna's best friend from high school invited to a New Year's party at her house.

A party. That's just what I need right now. Anna thought to herself.

She arrived at the party, dressed up in her favorite cocktail dress, wearing her best heels, hair tied up in a sleek bun and ready to take on the night. She mingled with all of her classmates from high school, everyone had so much going on, she thought. Some were pursuing a professional education;

some were working at their family businesses, and some had even gotten married or started a family. Meeting all of them felt refreshing to Anna.

She was sipping on her drink when she felt a gentle tap on the shoulder, it was a familiar face.

"Oh My God! Alex! It's been so long!", Anna called out in delight.

"Too long, if you ask me", Alex laughed as they embraced each other tightly.

"I am so glad you came today, I miss our time together, band practice, art class, everything…", Anna said smiling ear to ear.

"Me too, I see you're still as gorgeous as you were back in high school, maybe even more", Alex said as he stared into Anna's eyes gleaming with joy.

"Oh, c'mon you!", she playfully punched him.

The two disappeared from the crowd, catching up and reminiscing, as the new year dawned, bringing with it the fresh prospect of new beginnings.

Chapter 8: Finding Love

"**S**o, you're telling me, you haven't been on a date in almost a year?", Alex asked smirkingly.

"No, I really haven't, I've just been busy with school and the café, and I also went back to my folks for a while and stayed there", Anna replied.

Alex started frequenting the café at Anna's art school. He would often catch her at work and surprise her with flowers or take her out for lunch after her shift.

Alex stared longingly at her, how she had blossomed into a voluptuous woman. He ran his fingers through her hair and tucked it behind her ear.

"Anna you're so beautiful, you know, I always had a crush on you in high school, I mean, I kind of still do, I guess what I'm trying to say is, I always thought about asking you out but I didn't know how you might react and I didn't want to ruin our friendship, it just meant so much to me, but now that we've reconnected", he paused and stared at Anna, with a beaming face, who was listening attentively, her face flushing with blood, "All these feelings, they have come back and I don't want to waste any more time, so, do you want to be more than friends?".

Anna sheepishly smiled at him and started rummaging for words inside her head. She hugged Alex and said, "I always knew Alex, and you know how much I like you but…

"There's a but," Alex sighed.

"Yes, I am really sorry, but I don't think I can be in a relationship right now, I have been through so much in the past year, with my ex, it was just so messy, and I am still recovering from the aftermath of it all, just trying to put myself back together piece by piece, one day at a time", Hannah looked down despondently, "I am just not in the right head space to accommodate someone in my life right now, I want my next relationship to be a healthy one, whenever that happens, I hope you understand".

Alex's face changed. He spoke in a low, disheartened hum, "Okay, I understand, I hope that happens soon, you are over him Anna, you just need to try harder by being with someone new."

Hannah brushed it off without any delay by offering him a blueberry cupcake that had come fresh from the oven.

In the following week, Alex and Anna went to watch a movie together in an outdoor cinema. While the movie wasn't that great, Anna quickly found herself enjoying Alex's company. Maybe she was wrong about not giving him a chance? This date seems to have opened her eyes to a new possibility – the possibility of *finally* moving on and getting over John.

But was that even possible? Was she still in love with him or was it just an attachment she had? A connection that could never be broken no matter how hard she tried. But was love even necessary to be happy in a relationship? Could two people still be together even if one of them wasn't in love with the other?

Anna couldn't help but think about these things. She didn't understand why all of a sudden she was overthinking everything – about Alex, herself, John, and the future.

"Did you like the movie?" Alex asked, interrupting her thoughts.

"Oh, yes. I did," she said, smiling at him. Maybe he wasn't so bad and she would be really happy with him. There was *something* about him that gave some kind of reassurance that everything would be okay; like a soft hug on a cold winter day.

But everything that happened with John kept flashing before her eyes. She couldn't sleep at night without the help of sleeping pills or really dumb TV shows. She just wanted to get over him fast. Anna felt extremely depressed. She knew that John wasn't in her life anymore and wouldn't be with her, but she couldn't help but think about him all the time. There were days when all she wanted to do was be in his arms. But then there were days she felt anger towards him and wanted to do nothing with him. On those days, she would ground her teeth and scream into her pillow.

All the anger would come pouring out. Oh, how she hated what he had done to her! Oh, how she hated what he meant to her!

Days turned into weeks and before she knew it, the fire and rage inside of her started dwindling down. Perhaps, it was the fact that she had gotten tired of hating John. But at the same time, he was her *first kiss*. The first man she gave her heart to. How could she forget about him?

But she decided that waiting for him and getting closure was exhausting. So, in the coming weeks, when Alex asked her out again, she didn't hesitate to say yes.

Before she knew it, she had closed John's chapter in her book and turned a new leaf in her life. The way Alex made her feel was indescribable. She felt comfort but also felt uncomfortable. It was a feeling she couldn't comprehend.

She didn't understand what was going on inside her mind, but decided to ignore it.

Alex had gotten Anna a job at a marketing firm. And within months, Anna found herself successful. Her hard work paid off and she got promoted, allowing her to earn a handsome wage, enough to finally afford a house of her own.

All those years without John made her ask only one question: would she ever be able to forget about him?

Chapter 9: Breaking the Rose-Colored Glasses

"He is trying to gaslight you, Anna, please try to understand", Zara said concerningly.

"This is textbook psychological manipulation, and you must acknowledge it before it seriously affects you, as your healthcare professional, it is my duty to make you see the red flags", she explained to Anna.

"He's just distant, it's not manipulation, I'm sure there's an explanation for his behavior", Anna tried to make sense of it.

"He has kept you in the dark about his family and past relationships and whenever you question him, he starts to verbally abuse you, minimizes his own overreactions to every situation and completely shuts you out , until he realizes that he needs you in his life to feed his ego and his needs and then starts to love bomb you, making you think he values you and will not continue with his antics and yet tells you repeatedly that you are the sensitive one who overreacts to his abuse, tell me dear, how is this not manipulation?", Zara inquired starkly.

Anna had started to visibly shut down, she could not go through the whole cycle of abuse again. She just could not be stuck in a rut with another relationship. Her heart had already suffered too much.

Anna excused herself from Zara's office and hurried back to the firm. She spent the whole day lost in her thoughts until her friend asked her what was wrong.

"I don't trust this therapist, I think she's a nutcase herself, her words do not comfort me for one moment and I don't think I will visit her again", Anna said resolutely.

"She is a professional Anna, and she's absolutely right, I agree with her a hundred percent, and you should listen to her too, you must go back to her, hear her out and ask her how to deal with this situation. It's for your own good", her friend explained.

Anna took heed and decided to give Zara another chance. After all, she was the professional here, and Anna did not want to think she didn't try hard enough for herself.

Zara encouraged Anna to experiment with Alex on certain situations to become aware of his true intentions and feelings for Anna.

"You must corner him when he least suspects it, like at the end of the day, when you both are relaxing. Ask him about his whereabouts and see if he derails the conversation", Zara clarified.

Anna nodded in agreement and listened to her attentively. Her mind being completely observant and all her senses in alertness.

Zara continued to explain the telltale signs of gaslighting to Anna,

"You must recognize the signs immediately and write them down in a journal or the Notes app on your phone, there are things he would do or say that you must not ignore, things like, lying about or denying something and refusing to admit the lie even when you show him proof, insisting that an event or behavior you witnessed never happened and that you're remembering it wrong, he would even go as far as spreading rumors and gossip about you, or telling you that other people are gossiping about you, or he would just simply change the subject or refuse to listen when confronted about a lie, he would maintain his stance that you are the one who is overreacting and most importantly he would definitely try to smooth things over with loving words that don't match his actions".

"You should write this behavior down and then we shall discuss it in our next session", Zara intended.

Over the course of the next few weeks, Anna carried out those experiments on Alex that Zara had instructed her to do.

Alex would try to ice out Anna, but she would turn up at his work or repeatedly text him to meet with her. He would tell her she is becoming too clingy, and he needs some space to carry out his routine activities.

Days later, he would turn up at the firm and the two would get intimate, they would spend a few days together where Alex would ask Anna to stop meeting her friends and focus her time with him.

Anna would cautiously note his behavior and write it down in her Notes app, just like Zara asked. Other times she would delete the note and convince herself she is being neurotic and there is nothing devious about Alex's behavior. Anna's disbelief was getting stronger each day and she was adamant that this relationship of her, is authentic, Alex's feelings are valid, and that nobody could convince her otherwise.

Anna was spending entire days overplaying the incidents with Alex in her head. She was completely occupied with thoughts about him, whether his behavior with her was justified or not, did the situation demand it or was she just being a clingy girlfriend. Later, she would recall Zara's words and become suspicious of Alex and devise ways to confront him.

One night, completely exhausted by the constant battle with her thoughts, Anna decided to show up at Alex's house to confront him and put it all in open. She wanted to clear the air and talk things out with her boyfriend, after all they loved each other, what could possibly go wrong?

She had no idea.

Anna packed a change of clothes in her duffle bag, picked up Chinese food on the way to Alex's apartment. Anna had a key to his place and unlocked the door to see clothes lying on the floor. There were Alex's clothes and a lace teddy lying next to the sofa, it wasn't hers. She set the food down on the kitchen island and proceeded to look around in shock.

There were mumbled voices coming from the bedroom, but the door was shut. Anna barged in, panting heavily with tears running down her face. Only to discover Alex naked in bed with a blonde woman mounting him.

Anna felt dizzy, the rush of blood to her head was immense. She felt the entire apartment whirring. The veins in her temples started to throb. She tried to make her way out the front door but started to black out, tried to catch her balance but dropped on the living room floor, unconscious.

She later woke up on the couch in Alex's apartment, covered in a woolen blanket. She glanced around the apartment, there was no sign of the blonde woman.

"Anna you're up!", Alex showed up from the kitchen holding a mug of cocoa.

"Here, have some of this, you went completely pale", he handed her the mug and spoke so casually, like nothing had transpired a few hours ago.

Anna was hurting. And not just from the fall. She felt a sharp shooting pain in the middle of her chest.

"*Her*", she pointed to the room, her voice breaking, "*Who was she, Alex? Who was that woman you were fucking?* Now visibly shaking with rage.

"*That* was my girlfriend Claudia, I didn't expect you two to meet like this, I thought whenever it happened, it would be more civil", he joked nonchalantly.

"*You are a cheating pig!* You lied to me this whole time, I feel like a moron, a fool, I trusted you!", Anna got up, her face red and fuming, and slapped Alex.

Alex pushed her back to the couch, grinding his teeth in anger, "We never said we were exclusive Anna, this was never serious, Claudia is my coworker, we have been dating on and off before I met you at that party, so NO, I did not cheat on you!", he went on, "You are so messed up in the head, you have no sense of the world around you, you act like you are completely obsessed with me like a complete psycho! I have had enough of this".

"I've had enough of you!", Anna shrieked and dashed out of his apartment.

Anna returned to her house feeling hopeless and detached from the world around her. She had lost her faith in people. First, it was John who broke her heart, and now, Alex. She thought she didn't deserve this pain and wondered why it was always her who got betrayed like this. She was a good person; she had never wronged anyone.

It was too agonizing, all of it, she couldn't breathe and was choking on her own tears. Anna howled in pain. Her heart felt raw. She wanted to rip it out of her chest.

She could not go on like this, in fact, she could not go on anymore.

Chapter 10: No More

"**S**he's absolutely right!", Anna said to herself as she panted and stopped for a quick sip of water on her morning run.

She pulled out the earpiece from one of her ears. She was listening to the relationship podcast "Cut the Cord: How to Stop Being a Hopeless Romantic for Good" by an influencer called Maisie Sanders who gave young women relationship advice. Maisie was trending among single women with most women attributing their spiritual healing to her advice.

On this particular podcast, Maisie talked about how men are the reason women today suffer from mental health issues. She explained how women were suffering mentally and physically and if they wished to remain youthful and healthy, they must swear off men!

Anna had been listening to her podcast for the past six months, she was adamant that this woman made her see how useless men were and Anna could relate that to the men who had been in her life.

She had also been working out, going on hikes and runs and paying more attention to her physical wellbeing and diet.

Anna had completely cut herself off socially. She didn't go on any dates since her breakup with Alex. She didn't so much as engage in a conversation with any guy who showed interest in her. She just couldn't handle the heartache anymore, the incessant need for attention and love, the yearning for a guy who would not reciprocate her feelings, who would not show any commitment towards her. It made her feel smaller after each relationship ended. It made her feel insignificant and weak. She was ashamed of herself for putting her heart out on her sleeve only for someone to break it.

She had deleted all her accounts on dating sites, downright refused to go on blind dates and strictly told off her friends when they tried to hook her up with anyone. They wanted to help her but she dubbed them inconsiderate. Her phone barely got notifications anymore.

"We never see you anymore, Anna!", her friends complained.

"That's because I don't want to be seen or heard from again", Anna retorted, "Each time we see each other, you start to pry about my love life when you *know* how uncomfortable that makes me".

She deleted all the love songs on her playlist and contemptuously skipped every movie that would have even a tinge of romance. The sight of couples showing affection toward each other made her gag, she would rather watch taxidermy videos on YouTube.

Anna was done with it. With the pain and the suffering, the butterflies, and the longing. All of it. She wanted to set the butterflies on fire. She threw away everything that reminded her of her previous relationships, from presents to the dresses she had worn on dates. The paintings she used to make, trying to capture the moments she once thought she would cherish forever, she threw them in the trash. She didn't want to see any remnant of her misfortune in love.

She just wanted to move on in life. Her only relationship would be with her career, she thought. Her career wouldn't get up one day and decide to leave her shattered.

Anna directed all her focus towards work. She was quite literally entrenched in it. The job she had started out as an intern, she was now an associate there. She asked her boss to give her more responsibility so she could show the CEO the hard work she was putting in. She took on more projects and even worked at home, burning the midnight oil.

As time went on, Anna started to break ties with her friends. She would shrug them off for lunch meetups and tell them she's busy when they tried to visit her. She hadn't visited her hometown in over a year, she would occasionally pick up calls from her mother but completely ignored her father trying to reach her.

She received calls from Dr. Zara's office, getting reminders for her therapy appointments. She would tell them she is unavailable due to personal reasons. Anna's work projects occupied all her time. She didn't want to waste it on therapy and *after all what good had therapy done her?*

She had a strong grudge against Dr. Zara, not only for wasting her precious time and money, but for wrongfully making her believe she would get better. Anna thought she was a scam artist and that her license should be revoked. She had done more harm than good to her. Anna was left picking the pieces of her heart, all by herself.

The year went by, Anna found herself transformed into a completely different person from what she once used to be. She had become indifferent towards the world, nothing excited her anymore. Nothing except her work, it was the only driving force in her life.

Throughout this time, Anna had taken on projects that her superiors thought were far beyond her capability. But she proved them wrong. She proved her mettle and took on as much projects as she could. She brought the company a massive revenue by making deals with international clients and even volunteered to travel back and forth to several countries for her meetings.

Her tireless efforts did not go unrecognized. One day towards the end of the fiscal year, her boss called her in his office to give her some news.

"Anna the board of directors and I have seen your progress since you started here. We appreciate your hard work and untiring dedication towards our firm. If it were not for brilliant employees like you, we wouldn't be recognized internationally. So, to thank you, from the behalf of all of us, I want to offer you a promotion to Project Manager Marketing. I wish you all the success".

Anna couldn't believe her ears. She felt a robust sense of joy and relief flowing through her veins. She felt rejuvenated. Her hard work had paid off. Finally, a relationship that wasn't one sided. Her career.

It reaffirmed her belief that she only needed to focus on her career to thrive. She thought to herself,

I have cured myself of the heartache. I am on the right track. I found my calling; this is what I am supposed to do in life.

Chapter 11: On Fire

Anna stepped out of her navy-blue Mercedes Benz. She donned a white Gucci jumpsuit and beige Louboutin heels. She strutted down to the entrance of her favorite restaurant. The Maître d' recognized her immediately. It was an upscale restaurant that served on reservations only. But they knew Anna was a recurrent client. She always had her business meetings there. She called the restaurant her lucky charm because once she closed the deal there, the client would be in the palm of her hand.

She would order the most expensive champagne on the menu to tie it up in a neat little bow. Not only would she dazzle the client, but her track record impressed her colleagues as well. They were in awe of her. She had gained so much traction, so fast, but to Anna, it was all a blur. She was thriving on the excitement of it all. The adrenaline from each win would make her crave for more.

Anna was living lavishly; she began to wine and dine with the corporate elite. She would work late and catch Red Eye flights back to her penthouse apartment in the city. Lately, all Anna knew was work.

Anna hung her coat on a rack and slipped into a silk dress. She stood at the floor-to-ceiling windows of her luxurious penthouse apartment, gazing out at the city skyline. Flickering lights.

The room was spacious and modern, with sleek lines and a neutral color palette of cream and white. The floor was made of gleaming hardwood, with a plush cream-colored area rug that added a touch of warmth to the space.

In one corner of the room, there was a comfortable-looking leather sofa and armchair set in front of a large, flat-screen TV. A glass coffee table sat between them, surrounded by stacks of latest issues of business magazines and a vase of fresh flowers.

In the center of the room, a round glass dining table was surrounded by six white leather chairs. The table was set with sparkling crystal stemware and fine china, and a large orchid centerpiece graced its center.

The kitchen was a masterpiece of stainless steel and glass, with sleek cabinets and high-end appliances. A long, marble-topped island with a built-in sink and cooktop was perfect for preparing gourmet meals. Meals that Anna seldom made.

Down a hallway, there were two bedrooms, each with its own private bath. The first bedroom was decorated in soft pastels, with a plush king-sized bed and delicate lace curtains hanging from the windows. The second bedroom was more masculine, with a deep burgundy color scheme and a large, built-in bookshelf filled with books and other memorabilia.

Anna made her way to the roof deck, where a heated jacuzzi sparkled in the moonlight. She slipped into the water, feeling its warmth envelop her as she gazed up at the starry sky. She was living the life she had always dreamed of, and yet an emptiness overcame her.

She jumped out of the jacuzzi, the water dripping from her silk robe, tears running down her face. She felt trapped in her own body. She felt like an imposter.

Despite her impressive surroundings, she felt empty and unfulfilled. She felt lonely and miniscule. A certain darkness always lurked around her, no matter where she went.

She poured herself a glass of wine, but her thoughts kept drifting. She felt as though she was living someone else's life, a life that was expected of her rather than one that brought her joy. Her jaw started to stiffen up. The long hours and constant pressure to perform had taken a toll on her mental and physical health, and she was struggling to keep up the façade of perfection.

She put on a brave face, meeting with clients and attending business functions, but inside she was a mess. She had no time for hobbies or friends, and her relationships with loved ones had suffered. She felt trapped, unable to escape the cycle of work and stress.

She was tired all the time, with dark circles under her eyes and a constant headache, makeup could only cover so much. She found it hard to concentrate and remember things, and her mood swings were becoming more frequent and intense. Despite the obvious signs of burnout, she refused to slow down.

She told herself that she was tough, that she could handle anything that was thrown her way. But as the days passed, she was finding it harder and harder to keep up the pace. Her once-sharp mind was becoming muddled, and her normally-confident demeanor was faltering.

One day, during an important business meeting, she completely blanked and couldn't recall important details. She felt embarrassed and humiliated, but still refused to admit to herself that she was suffering. She pushed on, determined to keep up the appearance of success, no matter the cost.

But deep down, she knew that she was on a dangerous path, one that could lead to a complete breakdown if she didn't take action. Despite the obvious warning signs, she continued to ignore them, driven by her ambition and the fear of failure.

Her opulent apartment was a treat for the eyes, but it offered her no comfort. The spacious rooms and high-end furnishings only emphasized her loneliness and emptiness. She longed for true happiness, but it seemed just out of reach. Despite all of her success, she was silently suffering, feeling like a failure in the one area that mattered most - her own life.

One evening, Anna was perusing the aisles of the grocery store, her cart half-filled with items, when she heard someone calling her name. She turned to see her friend hurrying towards her, a look of concern on her face.

"Anna, I've been trying to reach you for weeks," her friend said, out of breath. "I was so worried when I couldn't get ahold of you. Are you okay?"

Anna sighed, feeling guilty for neglecting her friend. "I'm sorry, I've just been so busy with work."

"Busy? You look like you've been run over by a truck," her friend said, her tone worried. "You're pale, you've lost weight, and you look like you haven't slept in days. What's going on?"

Anna hesitated, not sure if she wanted to share the truth. But she found herself answering, "I'm just feeling overwhelmed," Anna admitted, her voice shaking. "There's so much pressure at work, and I can't seem to switch off. I'm always thinking about the next deadline or the next meeting."

Her friend nodded sympathetically. "You need to take care of yourself, Anna. You're pushing yourself too hard, and it's not healthy. What can I do to help?"

Anna blinked back tears, grateful for her friend's support. "I don't know, I just feel so lost right now. I don't know how to slow down, or even if I want to."

Her friend took her arm, giving it a reassuring squeeze. "Let's go back to your apartment, drop off the groceries, change into something fancy and let's go hit the bar for a drink or two. And I'm not taking no for an answer, okay? Anna managed and weak smile and nodded.

Anna's friend dragged her to the bar, drinks in hand, chatting about their lives. As they caught up, Anna opened up about Alex cheating on her, how John manipulated her and how she was struggling with anxiety trying to make sense of it all . She told her how she had been burying herself in work to avoid dealing with her emotions.

Her friend listened, her expression growing increasingly concerned. "Anna, I had no idea you were going through all of this," she said, her voice filled with sympathy. "You're carrying so much weight, and it's not healthy. You need to take care of yourself."

Anna nodded, feeling a sense of guilt. "I know, but I just feel like I have to keep going. Work keeps me busy, and I don't have to think about everything else."

"I understand that, but you can't keep running from your feelings forever," her friend said, her tone firm. "You need to give yourself time and space to process what you're going through, to heal and grow."

Anna sighed, feeling overwhelmed. "I don't know how to slow down. Work is my life, and I don't know how to find balance."

Her friend took a sip of her drink, looking thoughtful. "Maybe you can start by setting some boundaries. You could make time for self-care, like yoga or meditation, or therapy. And maybe you can find ways to work through your emotions, like journaling or taking an art class. The most important thing is to be kind to yourself, to give yourself grace and space to heal."

Anna promised her she would take out time for herself and work on healing herself from the wounds her past relationship had inflicted on her. They hugged and Anna returned to the comfort of her home.

Later that night, Anna lay in bed, staring up at the ceiling, unable to sleep. Her mind kept going back to her friend's advice, to the caution to take care of herself. Her mind kept racing back in forth, in loops. As she lay there, she began to recall the events that had led her to this point.

First, she remembered her painful breakup with John. He had used her innocence to manipulate her and left her feeling used and abused. He had made her feel special, made her pursue her passion for art. She had spent all that time waiting for him to come back to her. But it was to no avail. She had felt broken and vulnerable, and she had closed herself off from the world. She had forgone all hope for love and felt completely abandoned.

Then, Alex came into her life. She had let her guard down and given her heart to him, believed his empty promises, only for him to blatantly cheat on her, leaving her brokenhearted once again. The hurt and betrayal she had experienced from these two relationships had left her feeling as if she couldn't trust anyone and that love was nothing but a mirage.

It had driven her to throw herself into her work, to try and prove to herself and the world that she was more than just the sum of her heartbreaks. She had worked tirelessly, achieved great success, but all the while, she felt empty and alone.

Anna realized that her friend was right, and that her work had become her refuge, her means of escape from the pain of her past. But now, she saw that all of her achievements were meaningless if there was no one around to share them with. She needed meaningful connections, people in her life who cared about her, who supported her, who loved her. She didn't remember the last time she had laughed with her friends or had dinner with her parents. They didn't abandon her, yet she punished them for it. She had isolated herself from the people who did love her.

Her eyes welled up with tears as she realized the truth. She had been so focused on her career, on achieving success, that she had neglected what was truly important, and now she was feeling the consequences.

As the memories of heartbreak and pain flooded her mind, Anna felt herself being consumed by a darkness she had never experienced before. Her breaths grew shallow and rapid, her heart racing like a stampede of wild horses. The world around her started to spin and twist, as if she was stuck in a nightmare she couldn't escape.

With a Herculean effort, she reached for her phone and dialed 911. She could barely get the words out, gasping and choking on each breath as the panic attack took hold. The operator on the other end of the line tried to calm her down, but the storm inside her raged on.

As the ambulance screeched to a halt outside her apartment, Anna's vision started to fade. She felt herself being lifted onto a stretcher and whisked away, but everything was happening in a blur. The last thing she remembered was the sound of a paramedic's voice, calling her name in a desperate attempt to keep her conscious.

Then, the darkness consumed her.

Chapter 12: The End

Anna's eyes fluttered open, and she found herself in a sterile, white room. She was shell shocked. The walls were blank and devoid of any personal touches, and the harsh fluorescent lighting nearly blinded her. She covered her eyes for a moment and went back to scan the rest of the room.

The room that Anna was in, was small and sparsely furnished. It had a desolate, single, narrow bed pushed up against the wall, a small nightstand, and a plain wooden chair. The walls were stark white and bare except for a single, small window that let in a sliver of light. She heard mumbled voices coming from outside the room.

Anna looked down at herself. She was wearing a generic, hospital-issued gown. The fabric was rough against her skin. Her hair that used to always be freshly blown out was now disheveled, and she had dark circles under her eyes. No more concealer to hide them. A testament to the events that led her to this place. She felt dizzy and defeated, her once confident posture now slouched and fragile.

Her eyes were filled with a mix of fear and confusion, and her hands shook slightly as she clutched the thin blanket that was draped over her.

As she looked around in horror, she realized that she was in a mental hospital.

She felt a cold knot form in the pit of her stomach. This was not where she wanted to be. This was not what she had imagined for herself. She had worked so hard, fought so many battles, only to find herself in this place.

Tears streamed down her face as she took in the reality of her surroundings. The stillness of the room was oppressive, and the smell of disinfectant made her feel like she was suffocating. She felt disoriented and weak.

A familiar face made an entrance. They sat down on the singular wooden chair in the room. A red-haired woman with a poised demeanor. Her wavy locks framing her pale face. Clad in a moss green dress and a crisp white coat. Her crimson lips turned into a smile. A face she had dreaded and escaped from, for so long.

"I'm glad you're up", Dr Zara chimed.

Anna glanced at her in bewilderment.

"Dr. Zara," Anna said, her voice hoarse from disuse. "What are you doing here?"

Dr. Zara replied, examining the discomfort on Anna's face. "I've been keeping an eye on you since you were admitted here. How are you feeling?"

Anna took a deep breath and thought for a moment. "I'm... confused, I guess. Last, I remember I was home, in my bed, trying to sleep. I don't really understand what happened."

Dr. Zara nodded sympathetically. "It's normal to feel that way after experiencing a panic attack. But the important thing is that you're here and receiving treatment. I want to assure you that you're in a safe place and we're going to do everything we can to help you get better."

"I just feel so lost," Anna said, tears forming in her eyes. "I had everything under control and now I feel like it's all falling apart."

Noticing a distrust in her eyes, Dr. Zara tried to ease the tension, "I know it's been a long time since we've spoken, Anna. But I want you to feel comfortable talking to me. You know I'm here to help."

Anna hesitantly nodded, still feeling uneasy about the situation.

Dr. Zara continued, "I understand that you've been going through a lot lately. I know you've been struggling with anxiety and depression. I know you have been hiding behind your job to deal with it. That's why I want to help you work through these feelings. Continuing your therapy from where we left it off. You don't have to hide anymore Anna. It's okay, You're safe now."

Anna listened, trying to gather the courage to open up to Dr. Zara again, who waited patiently, allowing Anna to take her time. After a few moments of silence, Anna finally spoke up, "I feel like my life is falling apart. Everything I've worked so hard for, just doesn't seem to matter anymore. I want to know why it is always me holding the short end of the stick. I want to figure out why life has been so cruel to me. I did not deserve this pain, Dr. Zara. Please, help me make sense of it."

Dr. Zara nodded empathetically, "It's important to acknowledge that you're going through a tough time. It takes a lot of strength to face these feelings and seek help. It's okay to not be in control all the time, Anna. You have been so strong, fought so hard to deter your negative thoughts. But even strong people fall apart sometimes dear, you have been through so much."

She continued, "No, life has not been fair to you so far. But you are the only person who can change that. No romantic partner, or family member or friend can change that, Anna. It has always been you. The captain of your ship. You will have to believe that you can steer your ship in the right direction and regain control of your destiny and your happiness. I'm here to support you and work with you to help you regain your balance."

"I want to get better, I want to be able to truly live my life", Anna admitted hopefully.

Zara held her hand and smiled, "And you will, Anna. You just need to have a firm belief in yourself. You are such a gentle soul who knows only to give and never to take".

Anna started to sniffle, tears still streaming down her face.

"You must give yourself the love you keep trying to give everyone else. No one is more deserving of it than you. Once you start to love yourself, you will attract the people who appreciate you. You have to become your own happiness in order to draw it from the world around you. Enjoy your own company. Believe that you are deserving of all the good things in life. Believe that you are special, even if know one sees it. You must be the first person to acknowledge it and trust me, once you develop this mindset, the people around you will follow. They will see the light inside you. You burn so brightly, Anna, it's time you learn to shine for yourself."

The conversation continued, with Dr. Zara offering guidance and support to Anna as she opened up about her past year. Anna slowly began to feel more comfortable and at ease, knowing that she could finally trust someone to help her navigate her struggles.

As Dr. Zara finished speaking, Anna was enveloped by a tempest of emotions and thoughts. Her mind was ablaze with fear and disbelief, as she grappled with the realization that she had hit rock bottom.

The glittering lights, the awards, the promotions, the salary hikes - all of it seemed so trivial now, as she lay there in a mental hospital, staring at the sterile white walls. The life that she had meticulously crafted for herself was crumbling before her very eyes, leaving her with nothing but a hollow feeling in the pit of her stomach.

As memories from her past flooded her mind, Anna felt as if she was drowning in a sea of guilt and regret. The love she had foolishly given to those who did not deserve it, the moments she had sacrificed for the sake of her career, the relationships she had let slip away - all of it was weighing down on her like an anchor, pulling her under the surface.

She felt as though she was lost in a dense fog, unable to distinguish truth from fiction. Yet, amidst the turbulence of her thoughts, she knew one thing for certain - she couldn't continue down this path of self-destruction. The road ahead was uncertain, but she was determined to gather the courage to face her demons head on and reclaim the control that had eluded her for far too long.

In that moment, Anna was overwhelmed by the crushing emptiness of a life lived for the sake of appearances. The impeccable facade she had so carefully maintained was nothing but a mirage, and now, as she stared into the eyes of her therapist, she realized that there was no escaping the reality of her situation. It was time to face her demons, to confront the pain of her past, and to heal.

Anna felt consumed by an aura of enlightenment, basking in its radiance. She realized happiness was not a weight to be borne. It was meant to be felt, in the simplest of things. She felt immense gratitude for all the lessons she had learnt from heartbreak and compassion for the person she had once been. After all, she had survived the battles raging within her. She finally felt in harmony with her soul. With each breath, she felt her spirit soar, unencumbered by the shackles of the past. As she emerged from the depths of despair, she found solace in her own resilience and discovered the beauty of life that had been waiting for her all along. With each step forward, she was gifted with a brighter tomorrow, and she embraced it with a newfound sense of hope and renewal, transcending from a sunset to a sunrise.

Anna knew, that for the first time ever, her voice will not be silenced.

9 781961 028029